Caillou

Emma's Extra Snacks

Adaptation from the animated series: Anne Paradis
Illustrations taken from the animated series and adapted by Eric Sevigny
Content validation and poster: American Diabetes Association

Caillou was painting when he noticed Emma peeling
an orange.
"Snack time!" Caillou thought. He grabbed his lunch box
and sat down beside Emma.
"It's not snack time yet, Caillou," Miss Martin said.
"But Emma's eating her snack!" Caillou argued.
Miss Martin smiled. "Emma has permission to eat
extra snacks throughout the day," she said.

Caillou did not think it was fair that Emma got to eat
snacks when nobody else could.

"I can have extra snacks because I have diabetes,"
Emma said.

Caillou frowned at Emma. "What's diabetes?"

"That's a good question," Miss Martin said. "I think
it's time to explain it to the class."

"Emma recently found out that she has type 1 diabetes. It's an illness that some children and adults can get," announced Miss Martin.

"An illness that children can get?" The children were worried.

"Diabetes is not contagious, like the flu. You don't have to worry about catching it from Emma," Miss Martin added.

Clementine raised her hand. "What is diabetes?"
"Everyone has something called glucose in their blood,"
began Miss Martin. "It works like fuel for your body.
But sometimes Emma's blood doesn't have the right
amount of glucose."
Miss Martin showed them a gadget. "Emma uses this
to measure the glucose in her blood."
"It's called a blood glucose meter," added Emma.

Emma continued, "When I don't have the right amount of glucose in my blood, I take a medicine called insulin or sometimes I eat extra snacks! This way I don't feel dizzy or tired."

Miss Martin smiled. "Well done, Emma! Any questions, kids? Then it's time to go outside!"

Miss Martin made everything sound fine, but Caillou didn't feel fine. He was worried about his friend Emma.

The children were getting ready to go outside. Caillou grabbed Emma's sweater and handed it to her.
"You should wear this or you might catch a cold."
"I'll be okay, Caillou," Emma said.

In the playground, Caillou spotted Emma climbing the ladder to the slide. He rushed over and asked, "Do you feel dizzy, Emma? Do you want me to hold your hand?" She laughed and said, "I'm okay, Caillou."

The next day, Caillou was still worried about his friend. When he saw Emma carrying a big backpack, he ran to her. "Let me take this for you."

Emma replied, "I can carry my own bag."

"But it's too heavy!" Caillou insisted.

Emma gave him her bag and ran to meet the other children.

"Yay, it's track and field day!" The children were excited.
Miss Martin paired Caillou and Emma for a race.
Caillou thought, "I'll win for sure, and Emma will feel bad."
Miss Martin whistled. Caillou went slowly, but Emma took
off like a shot!
Caillou was surprised to see how fast Emma ran. So he
ran faster to catch up to her.

"It's a tie!" cried Miss Martin. Caillou and Emma were trying to catch their breath.

"You sure don't act sick!" Caillou said.

"Sick? I'm not sick," replied Emma.

"But you've got type 1 diabetes!"

"Yes, but I'm still just like you, Caillou. It's just something I have to live with."

Caillou was stunned. "Every day?" he said.

Emma nodded.

Emma showed Caillou the gadget clipped to her pocket.
"This pump gives me insulin so I feel well. I check my
blood glucose a lot, and the snacks help too."
Caillou was impressed with his friend. Emma did
so many things to take care of herself.
Caillou felt less worried.

"Do you feel dizzy now, Emma?" Caillou asked.
She shook her head.
"Then I'll race you again!"
Caillou started to chase Emma around the playground.
He was happy that his friend could play with him.
Emma had to live with diabetes, but she could still have lots of fun just like other kids do.

CAILLOU is a registered trademark of Chouette Publishing (1987) Inc.
DHX MEDIA is a registered trademark of DHX Media Ltd.

Text: adaptation by Anne Paradis of the animated series CAILLOU,
produced by DHX Media Inc.
All rights reserved.
Original script written by Sheila Dinsmore.
Original episode #16B-518C Emma's Extra Snacks
Illustrations: Eric Sévigny, based on the animated series CAILLOU

The PBS KIDS logo is a registered mark of PBS and is used with permission.

We acknowledge the financial support of the Government of Canada through
the Canada Book Fund for our publishing activities.

Canadian Patrimoine
Heritage canadien

We acknowledge the support of the Ministry of Culture and Communications
of Quebec and SODEC for the publication and promotion of this book.

SODEC
Québec

Bibliothèque et Archives nationales du Québec and Library and Archives
Canada cataloguing in publication

Paradis, Anne, 1972-
Caillou, Emma's Extra Snacks
(Playtime)
For children aged 3 and up.

ISBN 978-2-89718-205-2

1. Diabetes - Juvenile literature. I. Sévigny, Éric. II. Title. III. Title: Emma's
Extra Snacks. IV. Series: Playtime (Montréal, Québec).

RC660.5.P37 2015   j616.4'62   C2015-940246-8

Printed in China
10 9 8 7 6 5 4 3 2 1 CHO1938 MAY2015